# The Berenstain Bears'® STORYTIME COLLECTION

## 10 Beloved Stories

By Stan & Jan Berenstain

Random House New York

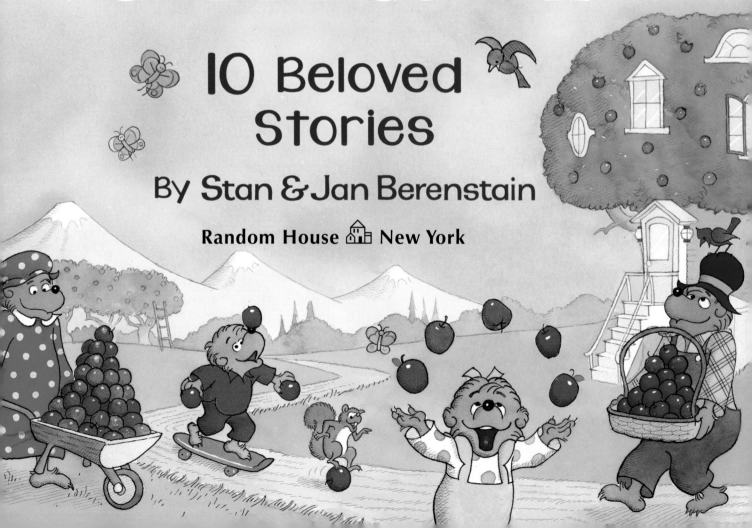

All rights reserved. Published in the United States by Random House Children's Books, a division of Penguin Random House LLC, New York. The stories in this collection were originally published separately in the United States by Random House Children's Books, New York, as *The Berenstain Bears' New Baby* in 1974, *The Berenstain Bears Go to School* in 1978, *The Berenstain Bears and the Sitter* in 1981, *The Berenstain Bears Go to the Doctor* in 1981, *The Berenstain Bears Visit the Dentist* in 1981, *The Berenstain Bears' Moving Day* in 1981, *The Berenstain Bears Get in a Fight* in 1982, *The Berenstain Bears Go to Camp* in 1982, *The Berenstain Bears in the Dark* in 1982, and *The Berenstain Bears and the Messy Room* in 1983.

Random House and the colophon are registered trademarks of Penguin Random House LLC.

Visit us on the Web!
rhcbooks.com
BerenstainBears.com

Educators and librarians, for a variety of teaching tools, visit us at RHTeachersLibrarians.com

ISBN 978-0-593-17732-7
Library of Congress Control Number: 2020935032

MANUFACTURED IN CHINA
10 9 8 7 6

# CONTENTS

# The Berenstain Bears'
# NEW BABY

## Stan & Jan Berenstain

Down a sunny dirt road, over a log
bridge, up a grassy hill, deep in Bear
Country, lived a family of bears—
Papa Bear, Mama Bear, and Small Bear.

They lived in a large tree which
Papa Bear had hollowed out and
made into a house.

It was a very fine house.
This is what it looked like inside.

13

It was fun growing up in Bear Country . . .

helping Papa get honey from the old bee tree . . .

helping Mama bring the vegetables
in from the garden.

There were all sorts of
interesting things for a
small bear to do and see
in Bear Country.

Small Bear felt good growing up
in a tree . . . in his own room . . . in the
snug little bed that Papa Bear had made
for him when he was a baby.

But one morning, it did not feel
so good. Small Bear woke up with
pains in his knees and aches in his legs.

"Small Bear, you have outgrown
your little bed," said Papa Bear, as he
hitched up his overalls and buttoned
his shoulder straps.

"Today, we shall go
out into the woods and
make you a bigger one!"

With that, he ate his breakfast of piping-hot porridge . . .

washed it down with a gulp of honey from the family honey pot . . .

took up his ax and was
out the door.

"But, Papa," called Small
Bear, following after him.
"What will happen to my
little bed?"

23

"Don't worry about that,
Small Bear," said Mama Bear
as she closed the door after him.

24

She smiled and patted her front, which had lately grown very big and round.

"You've outgrown that snug little bed just in time!"

"What will happen to my little bed?" Small Bear asked as he caught up with Papa Bear. But Papa was sharpening his ax on his grinding stone and didn't hear.

"Yes, indeed," said Papa Bear. "You need a bed you can stretch out in—a bed that will not give you pains in your knees and aches in your legs."

He tested
the ax to see
if it was sharp,

then headed off
into the woods.

"What will happen to my little bed?"
Small Bear asked again as he caught up with
Papa Bear in the woods. Papa had chopped
down a tree and was splitting it into boards.
"We will have a new baby soon
who will need that little bed,"
said Papa Bear as he whacked
off another board.

"A new baby?" asked Small Bear.
(He hadn't noticed that Mama Bear had
grown very round lately, although he
*had* noticed it was harder and harder
to sit on her lap.)

"And it's coming soon?"

"Yes, *very* soon!" said Papa Bear.

With a final whack he split off the last
board, which gave him enough wood to
make a bigger bed for Small Bear.

They made the bed a good size
and took the rest of the day to
chip and shave it smooth and neat.
Then they carried it back to
the tree and up to Small Bear's room.

When they got there, Small Bear noticed right away that his old bed wasn't there anymore.

"My little bed!" said Small Bear. "It's already gone!"

"You outgrew it just in time," called Mama Bear from the next room. "Come and see."

It was true! There was his snug
little bed with a new little baby in it.
    Small Bear had outgrown his snug
little bed just in time for his new baby
sister. And now *he* was *a big brother*!

She was very little but very
lively. As Small Bear leaned over
for a closer look, she popped him
on the nose with a tiny fist.

"Hmm," said Small Bear. "She has a pretty good punch for a little baby."

That night he stretched out proudly in his bigger bed.

"Aah!" he said. "Being a big brother is going to be fun."

The next morning he woke up feeling fine, with no pains in his knees or aches in his legs.

His nose was a little tender, though.

# The Berenstain Bears

# Go to School

Stan & Jan Berensta

When summertime ends
and the weather turns cool,
most little bears
are ready for school.....

It had been a wonderful summer for the Bear family. They had gone swimming and boating at the lake. They had picnicked in the woods and taken many walks along sunny paths.

But now summer was just about over. There was a nip
in the air. The birds were beginning to fly south,
and the leaves on the tree house were changing colors.

One evening at supper, Brother Bear said, "I'm getting tired of summer vacation. I think I'm ready to go back to school!"

"That *is* good news," said Papa Bear. "Because school will be starting again, very soon!"

Sister Bear's ears perked up at the word *school.*

Mama Bear noticed. "As a matter of fact," she said, "Sister and I are going to meet her new teacher tomorrow."

This year Sister would be starting kindergarten. And she wasn't quite sure how she felt about it.

43

She liked being at home
with her mother and father...

her books and toys...

and all her friends.

"What will school be like, Mama?" she asked at bedtime.

"You'll find out tomorrow," said Mama as she tucked Sister in and kissed her good night.

The next day, Mama and Sister packed a lunch and took the long walk down the winding dirt road to the Bear Country School.

Handybear Gus was up on a ladder, fixing the roof.

"Hello!" said Mama. "This is Sister Bear. She starts kindergarten next week."

"We'll be glad to have her," said Gus.
"Miss Honeybear is the kindergarten teacher.
You'll find her inside."

"Hello there!" said Miss Honeybear in a loud, jolly voice. "Come right in and look around!"

Sister thought Miss Honeybear's voice was a little scary. But she let Miss Honeybear take her hand and lead her into the kindergarten room.

What a big, friendly room! It had yellow
curtains and tables and chairs that looked
just right for someone Sister's size.

"What do you *do* in kindergarten?"
Sister asked as they sat down for lunch.

"We read stories, sing songs, learn our
ABCs, paint pictures, play games, make things
out of clay, build with blocks—we do *lots* of
things!" said Miss Honeybear.

Those were all things Sister liked to do.
And she had never seen such big jars of paint...
or such fine blocks. There was even a whole
barrel of clay....

School might be fun, after all, thought Sister
by the time she and Mama started home.

But when the big morning came, Sister began to worry again. "Mama!" she said. "What if I don't like school? What if I just don't like it?"

Just then the big yellow school bus
pulled up to the tree house.

"Stop worrying!" said Brother Bear.
"School is fun. You'll like it. Now let's get going
or we'll miss the bus!"

He grabbed her hand and away they went.

Every so often the bus stopped and more bears climbed on.

Most of them were excited like Brother. But some of the smaller ones were quiet like Sister.

As more and more old friends climbed on, they got noisier and noisier... and the smaller ones got quieter.

The little bear who sat
next to Sister began to look
worried, so she smiled
at him and held his hand.

At last the bus arrived. The Bear Country School looked very nice. Handybear Gus had fixed the roof, and painted the trim, and cut the grass.

And Miss Honeybear's kindergarten room looked beautiful. Everything was ready!

Bee

Cat

Before very long, the kindergartners got noisy! Two of them wanted to play with the same dump truck. Two others wanted to look at the same book. And a whole gang of them wanted to be first to play with the blocks. What a commotion!

Suddenly a loud, jolly voice called out: "Storytime!" Miss Honeybear was calling the class to the book corner. *That* quieted things down.

After the story, Sister tried
everything. She painted a picture...

helped build a block city...

made a giant clay doughnut...

and looked at the books.

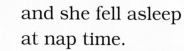

She ate all of her bread and
honey at snack time...

and she fell asleep
at nap time.

When she climbed off the bus
with Brother at the end of the day,
Sister was the excited one.

"Mama! Papa! Look what I did
in school today!" she said, holding
up her painting.

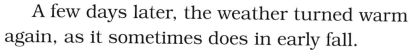

A few days later, the weather turned warm again, as it sometimes does in early fall.

Brother was restless at breakfast. "I wish it was still summer vacation," he said, "so I wouldn't have to go to school today."

"Oh, come on, Brother Bear!" said Sister. "School is fun. Let's get going or we'll miss the bus!"

On the bus, all the bears were talking about the things they were going to do at school—soccer practice, science projects, music lessons—all kinds of things!

Hmm, thought Brother. Sister Bear was right. School *is* fun!

And off they went in the big
yellow bus to the Bear Country
School.

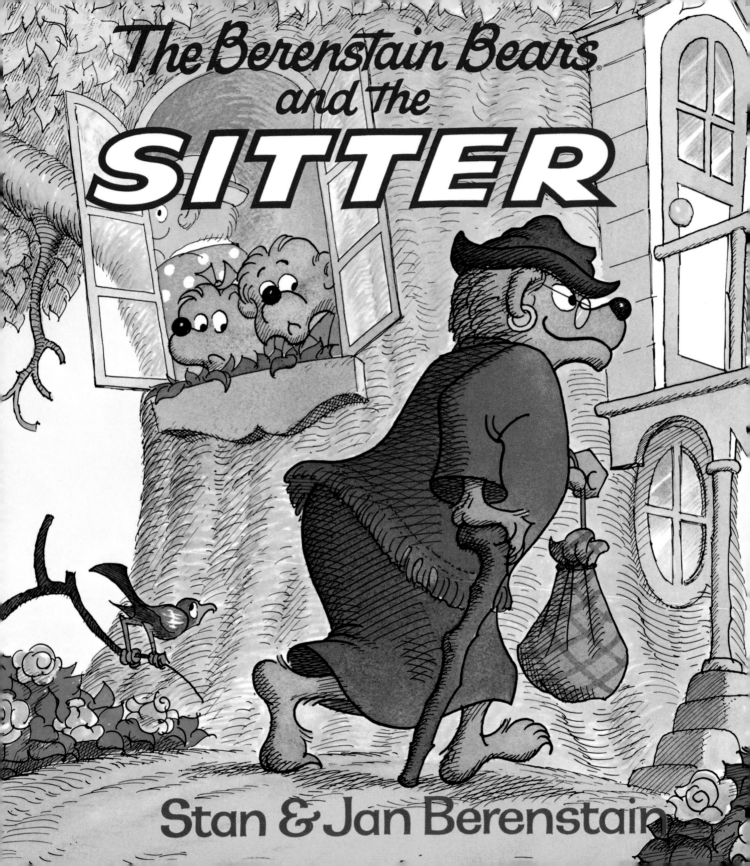

"What's this?" said Papa Bear, as he took the day's mail from the Bear family's mailbox.

It was a notice telling about an important meeting that night at the Bear Country Town Hall.

Mama Bear called up Grizzly Gran.
Brother and Sister Bear sometimes
stayed with Gramps and Gran when
Mama and Papa Bear had to be away.

But Gramps and Gran were planning to go to the meeting, too. So Brother and Sister couldn't stay with them.

Or with Aunt Maude...

or Cousin Wilbur.
They were going to the
meeting, too.

"Why can't we go with you?" asked Sister, beginning to get a little upset.

"Yeah!" added Brother Bear.

"Because," said Papa, "this meeting is for grown-ups. And, besides, it won't be over until late—way past your bedtime."

"Well, where are we going to stay?" the cubs wanted to know.

"You're going to stay right here,"
said Mama, as she put down the phone.

"Alone?" asked Sister.

"Of course not," said Mama.
"I've arranged for a sitter."

"A sitter?!" said Brother.

"Who is it going to be?"
Sister asked.

"Mrs. Grizzle, who lives
in the hollow stump at the
end of the road," said Mama,
feeling much better about
the whole thing.

"Mrs. Grizzle!" said the
cubs, not feeling better
at all. . . .

Once, when Sister was playing with her friends, their ball went into Mrs. Grizzle's flower garden.

Mrs. Grizzle wasn't too happy about it.

And another time, when Brother was flying his kite, it swooped and bumped Mrs. Grizzle on the hat.

She wasn't too tickled about that, either.

Later that evening, after the supper things had been cleaned up, Mama and Papa got ready to go to the town meeting.

"But who's going to scrub our backs, read us a story, and tuck us in?" asked Sister, still a little nervous about the idea of a sitter.

"I understand that Mrs. Grizzle has raised seven cubs of her own," said Mama, putting on her hat. "And I'm sure she's a perfectly good back scrubber, story reader, and tucker-inner."

"She's not going to scrub *my* back!" Brother Bear said under his breath.

Mrs. Grizzle came walking up the path to the Bears' tree house right on time.

There was no question about it. It was the same Mrs. Grizzle who got bopped with the kite and didn't like cubs tromping her flowers.

She was very large—almost as big as Papa— and she carried a drawstring bag.

"Evenin', all!" said Mrs. Grizzle in a loud, jolly voice. "Well, time's a-wastin', you two!" she said to Mama and Papa. "You better skedaddle off to your meetin'!"

Mrs. Grizzle had a strong way of saying things, and folks usually did what she said.

Mama and Papa kissed the cubs good night—and skedaddled.

"Whew!" said Mrs. Grizzle, as she sat down in Papa's big chair. "It sure is good to get a load off your feet!" She took off her hat and looked into her drawstring bag.

There's something about somebody looking into a bag that makes cubs very curious.

"Mrs. Grizzle?" said Sister.

"Yes?"

"What's in the bag?"

"Nothin' much. Just some things I take along when I go sittin'—a piece of string, a pack of cards . . ."

Meanwhile, over at the Town Hall, the bears were getting ready for their important meeting.

They were getting ready for speeches, voting, and arguments about some new laws.

But Mama's mind was not on the meeting. Neither was Papa's. Mama and Papa Bear were thinking about what was going on back home.

"Sister looked a little worried when we left," fretted Mama.

"So did Brother," agreed Papa.

They decided to call home and see how things were going.

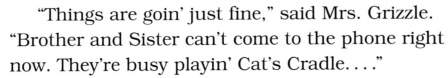

"Things are goin' just fine," said Mrs. Grizzle. "Brother and Sister can't come to the phone right now. They're busy playin' Cat's Cradle...."

"Have a good meeting!" shouted the cubs.

"—But they say to have a good meetin'!"

After Cat's Cradle, they played Go Fish with the cards that came out of Mrs. Grizzle's drawstring bag.

Then they played Tiddlywinks with a special set of winks that Mrs. Grizzle had made out of polished stones and a snail-shell cup.

After a while, the cubs got the
yawns, and Mrs. Grizzle began getting
them ready for bed.

And she did, indeed, turn
out to be a very good back
scrubber (Brother changed
his mind about not having
his back scrubbed). . . .

And she was
a fine story reader . . .

and a really super
tucker-inner.

"I hope Mama and Papa had a good meeting," said Sister with a yawn, "because we had a very good sit."

The cubs had a number of different sitters from time to time, but Mrs. Grizzle was their favorite—and they were always glad to see her.

# The Berenstain Bears® GO TO THE DOCTOR

Stan & Jan Berenstain

Take a deep breath.
Stick out your tongue.
Come see Doctor Grizzly
While you are young.

"Tomorrow," said Mama Bear as she helped the cubs get ready for bed, "you'll be going to the doctor for a checkup."

"Doctor?" said Brother Bear. "We're not sick!"

"And what's a checkup?" asked Sister Bear, a little worried.

"It's just what it sounds like," said Mama. "Dr. Grizzly will check to see if you are growing the way healthy cubs should."

"Will it hurt?"
asked Sister, pulling
the covers up close.

"Now, now," said Papa Bear as he kissed her good night. "You just settle down. There's absolutely nothing to worry about."

But Sister wasn't so sure.

The next morning, after a good breakfast, the family got into their red roadster and were on their way.

"Do you ever get checkups, Mama?"
Sister asked as they drove along the
dusty dirt road.

"Yes, I do," answered
Mama.

"*I* don't need checkups
anymore," bragged Papa.
"Because I...I...

--AH-CHOO!

...never get sick."

"That was quite a sneeze," said Mama.

"It's this dusty road," said Papa, turning onto the main highway into Beartown.

They pulled to a stop in front of the
doctor's office.

"Come, cubs!" said Mama. "We don't want
to be late for our appointment."

But Brother held back. He remembered
something.

"Are we going to get shots?" he asked.

"That's up to...to... to...

–AH-CHOO!

...the doctor," said Papa, sneezing an even bigger sneeze than before.

"Bless you!" said Mama.

"It's just this bright sunlight," sniffed Papa.

"I *never* get sick."

The doctor's waiting room was a busy,
cheerful place with pictures on the
walls, books to look at, and puzzles
to do. Brother started a puzzle. Sister
took a book, but didn't really look at it.
Other bears were coming in—and she
looked around the room at them. There
were cubs of all ages with their parents.

Some of the smallest cubs looked a little worried. Sister smiled at them so they wouldn't be afraid.

There was a big cub with a cast on his leg. It had names and funny drawings all over it.

He let Brother write his name on it for luck, and Sister drew a picture.

There was even a little baby cub only a few weeks old.

"Next!" called Dr. Grizzly. It was Brother's and Sister's turn.

Dr. Grizzly was friendly, but she got right down to work. She had a lot of bears to take care of and not much time to waste.

First, she weighed and measured the cubs.

"Fine!" she said. "You've both gained weight nicely and grown taller."

She listened to their chests with a stethoscope.

And poked them all over to check on everything inside.

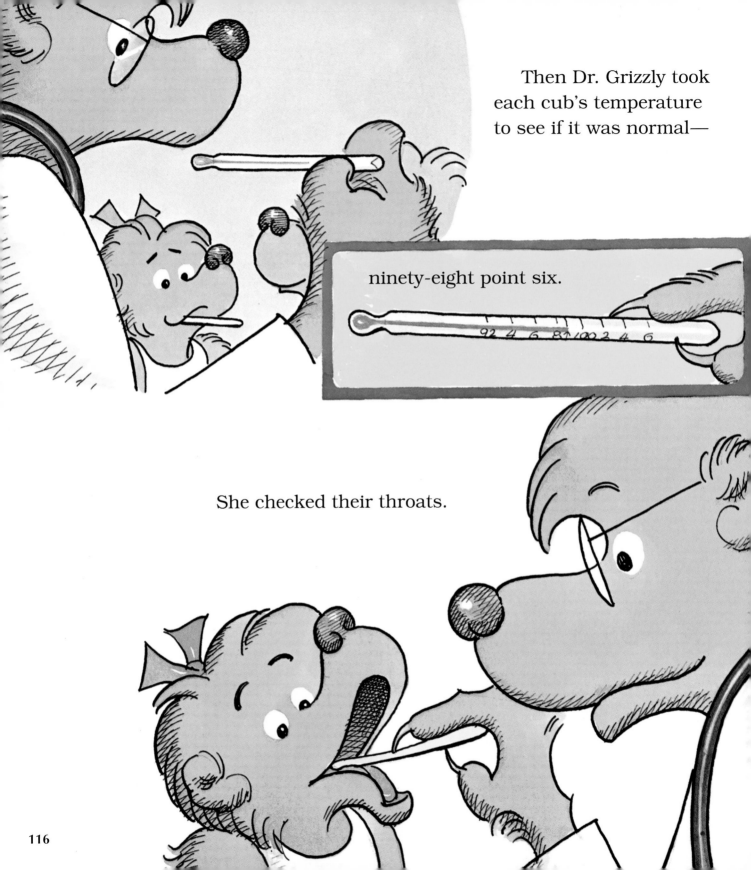

Then Dr. Grizzly took each cub's temperature to see if it was normal—

ninety-eight point six.

She checked their throats.

Then she looked at their eyes,

ears,

and noses with a
special little light.

Next, she tested their hearing
by whispering very softly.

Then came the eye test. Brother read every letter except the very smallest. Sister didn't know all the letters yet, so she read a special chart that looked like this:

"Very good!" said the doctor as she studied some papers in a folder.

Sister whispered to Brother, "So far, it hasn't hurt at all!"

"Well, that pretty much takes care of it," said
Dr. Grizzly, looking through her eyeglasses
at the papers, "except for one thing. I see it's time for
your booster shots."

"I knew it!" said Brother.

"Why do we have to have shots when we're not even
sick?" said Sister.

"Now, Sister," said Papa, "the doc . . . doc . . . doc . . .
AH-CHOO! . . . doctor knows best!"

"Bless you," said Dr. Grizzly. "And that's a very
good question, Sister. . . ."

As she got the shots ready, she called out into the
waiting room, "I've got a brave little cub in here who's
going to show you all how to take a shot!"

121

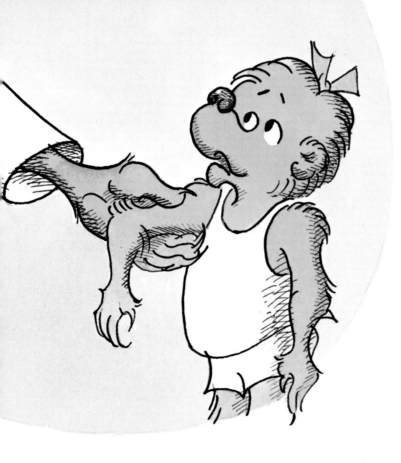

"Getting back to your question, Sister," said Dr. Grizzly. "You see, there are some kinds of medicine that you take after you get sick, and those are very useful. But this kind of shot is a special medicine that keeps you from *getting* sick."

"Will it hurt?" asked Sister.

"Not nearly as much as biting your tongue or bumping your shin," the doctor explained. "There! All done!"

Dr. Grizzly was right! And it happened so fast that Sister didn't even have time to say ouch!

The little cubs who were watching were *very* impressed.

So was Brother.

After Brother's shot, Papa said, "Well, Doctor, we'll be go...go...go...

. . . going now."

"Just a minute, Papa Bear," said Dr. Grizzly.
"Let me have a look at you."

"But I *never* get sick . . . ," Papa started to say.

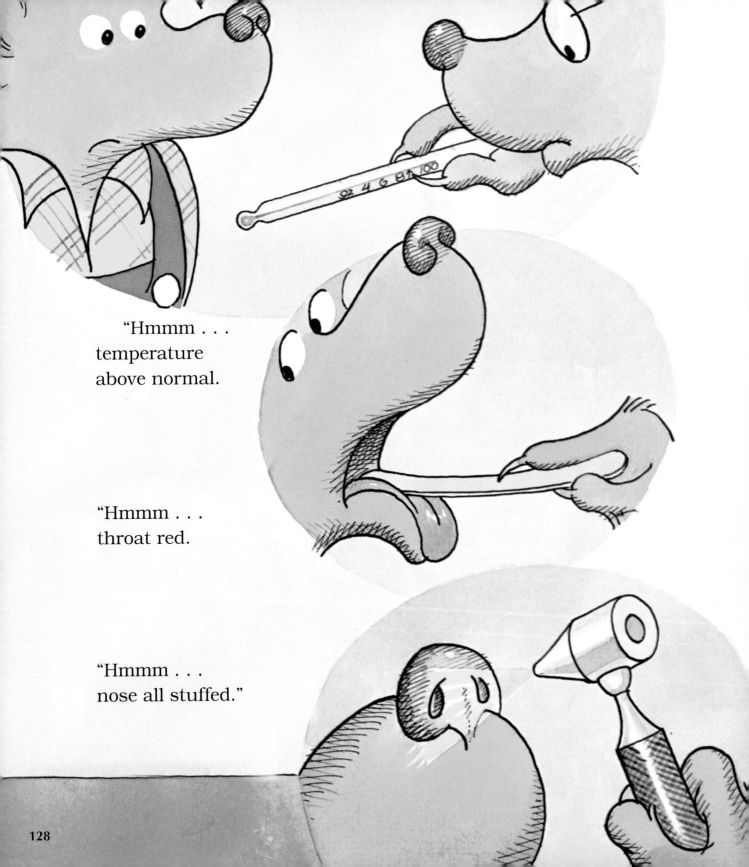

"Hmmm . . .
temperature
above normal.

"Hmmm . . .
throat red.

"Hmmm . . .
nose all stuffed."

"Time for your medicine, Papa!" said the cubs, offering him a big spoonful of the gooey pink stuff that Dr. Grizzly prescribed for his cold.

"Well," said Papa, smiling weakly, "I *hardly* ever get sick!"

# The Berenstain Bears
# VISIT THE DENTIST

## Stan & Jan Berenstain

Taking good care of their teeth
Is something all bears do.
That's why Sis and Brother brush—
And go to the dentist, too.

One morning, Sister Bear woke up in the same old bed, in the same old pajamas, and yawned the same old yawn. But something was different.

"I have a looth tooth," she told Brother Bear.

133

"Well, push it back and forth with your tongue, and maybe it'll come out," yawned Brother, as he turned over to go back to sleep.

"Then what?" asked Sister. Brother had told her about the tooth fairy, and she wanted to hear it again.

"Then, put it under your pillow, and the tooth fairy will take it away and leave a new coin in its place. . . ."

"But," Brother added, "be sure to tell Mama about it first!"

Later, at breakfast, when Mama was reminding Brother that he had a dentist's appointment after school, she noticed that Sister was eating funny.

"She has a loose tooth," Brother explained.

"When it comth out," said Sister, wiggling it with her tongue, "I'm going to put it under my pillow for the tooth fairy."

"If she doesn't wiggle it out, she can come to the dentist with us and he can *yank* it out!" Brother grinned.

"Never mind that kind of talk," said
Mama. "Dr. Bearson doesn't yank. He's
very gentle and very careful."

"I'll get it out myself,
Thmartie!" Sister shouted,
as Brother hopped onto the
big yellow school bus.

But Sister was still wiggling her loose tooth with her tongue when she and Mama met Brother after school and went to the dentist.

141

"Ith thtill thtuck," she said, showing Dr. Bearson her loose tooth.

"Well," said the dentist, "I'll have a look at it after I examine Brother's teeth. You can stand on this stool and watch—if that's all right with Brother."

"Sure," said Brother, as he climbed into the special cub's seat in the big dentist's chair. "She can watch me and see how it's done."

Brother had been to the dentist before, and he couldn't help showing off just a little.

Sister watched as Dr. Bearson checked each one of Brother's teeth with a special little tool.

"How do you see the backs?" she asked.

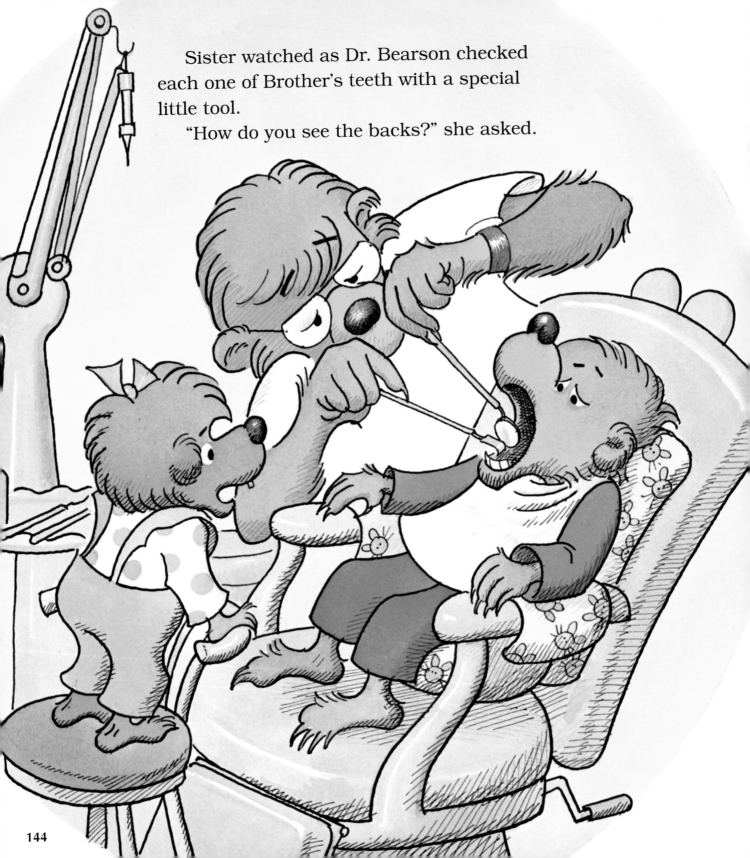

"With this little mirror," said the dentist. "Here. Have a look."

"Wow!" said Sister, looking into Brother Bear's mouth. "It looks like a cave. A cave with a tongue!"

While Dr. Bearson checked
Brother Bear's teeth, Sister
looked at the other tools on his
work tray—there were . . .

little picks, a scraper . . .

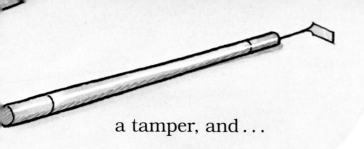

a tamper, and . . .

ULP!—a yanker!

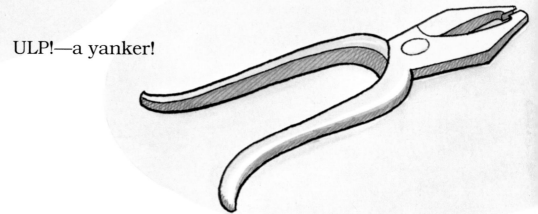

She had become so interested
that she had forgotten all about
her loose tooth! She went to work
wiggling again. She wiggled hard.
But it was still stuck.

147

There were some other interesting
dentist's things:

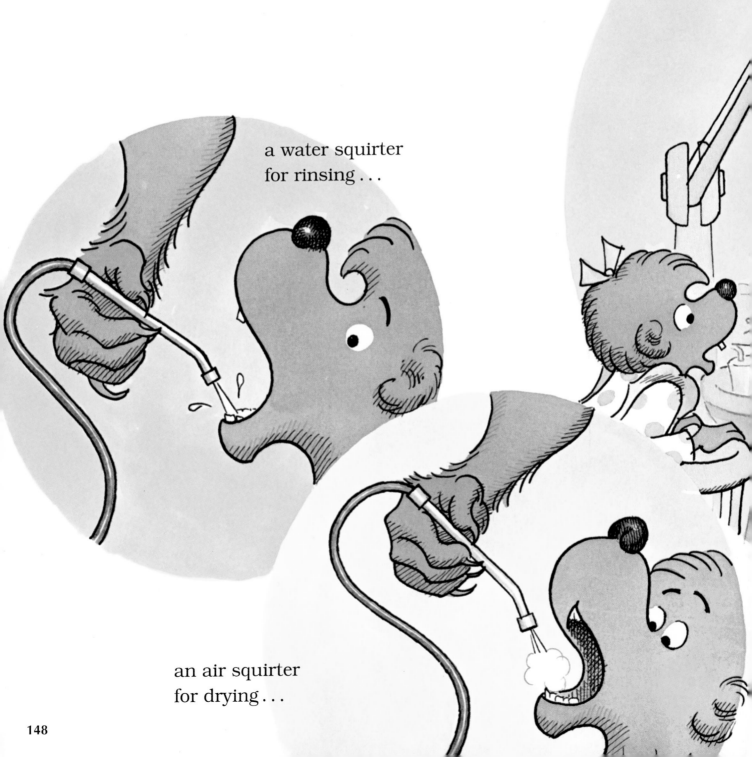

a water squirter
for rinsing . . .

an air squirter
for drying . . .

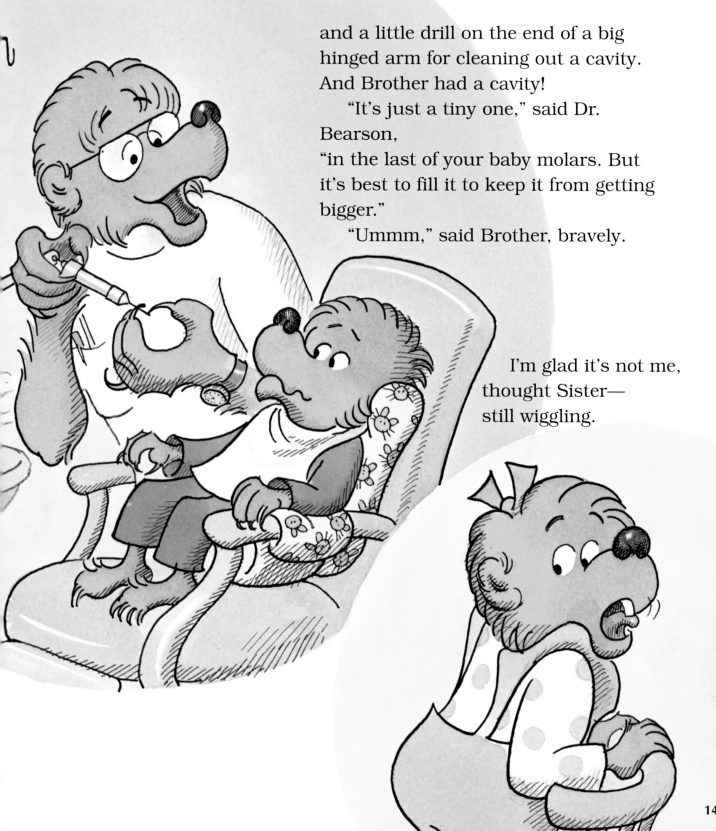

and a little drill on the end of a big hinged arm for cleaning out a cavity. And Brother had a cavity!

"It's just a tiny one," said Dr. Bearson,
"in the last of your baby molars. But it's best to fill it to keep it from getting bigger."

"Ummm," said Brother, bravely.

I'm glad it's not me, thought Sister—
still wiggling.

After Dr. Bearson cleaned out the cavity,
he rinsed it with the water squirter and
dried it with the air squirter.

Then he mixed up some
filling cement . . .

and filled it.

He gently tamped the filling down and scraped it smooth. A final rinse, and Brother jumped down—as good as new.

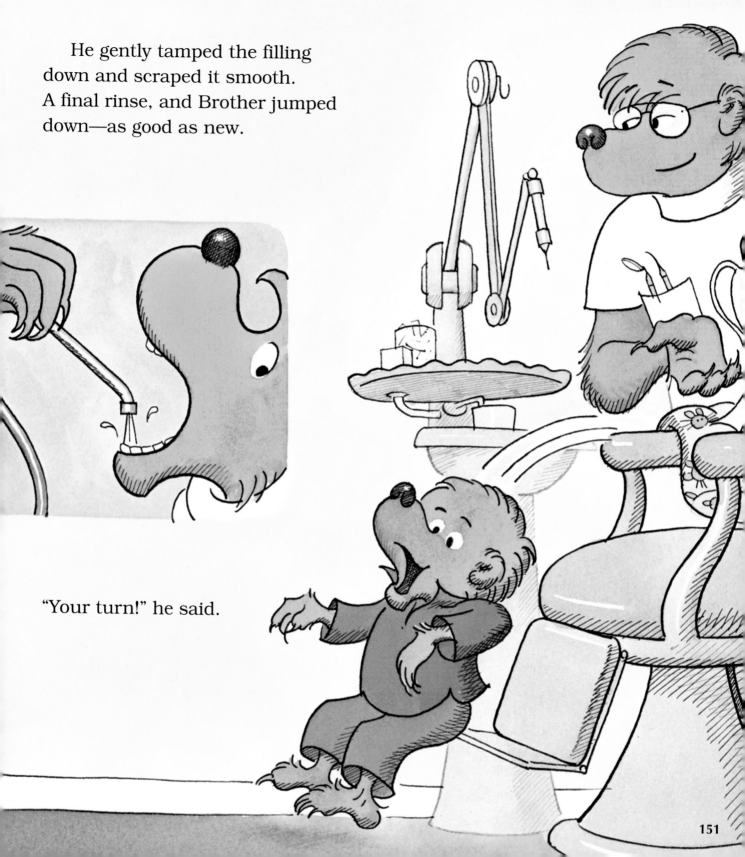

"Your turn!" he said.

Bravely, Sister climbed up into the cub's seat—still wiggling, but that loose tooth just didn't seem to want to come out.

"Hmmm," said the dentist, looking at the tooth.

"Ulp!" said Sister, waiting for him to reach for those big yankers. But while she waited, Dr. Bearson gripped the tooth with a piece of gauze, gave a tug, and . . .

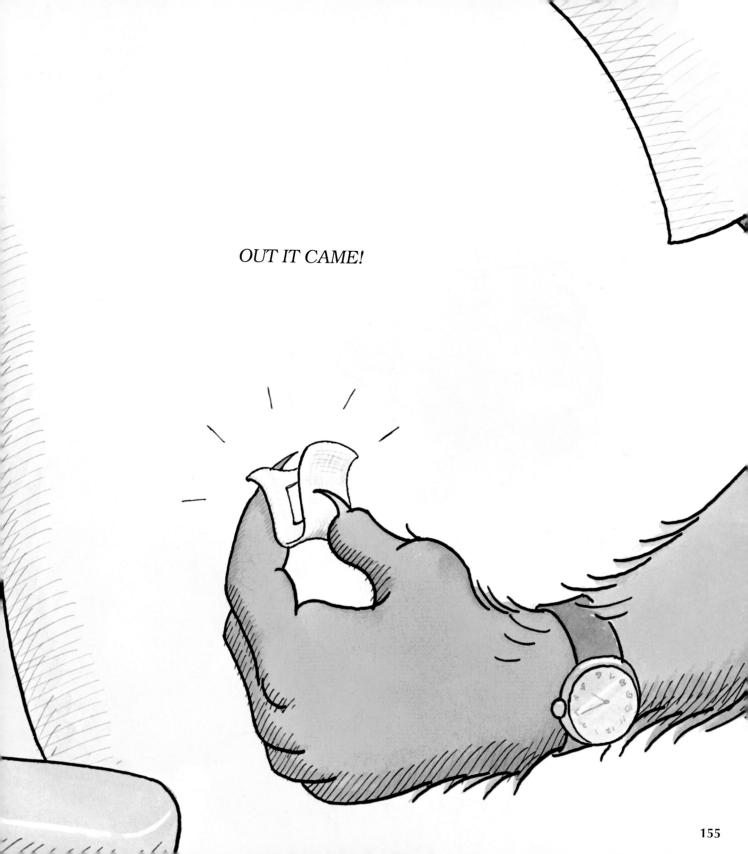

OUT IT CAME!

Sister looked at the tooth. It was very tiny. Dr. Bearson gave it to her to keep. Now it was her turn to hop down as good as new.

"Don't I get a lollipop or something for being good?" she asked Brother.

"You get a balloon," he said. "Lollipops aren't good for your teeth."

I BRUSH EVERY DAY

DR. BEARSON DENTIST

The next morning, Sister plunged her hand under her pillow and found a shiny new dime where the tooth had been.

"The tooth fairy came!" she told Brother.

"I told you she would," he yawned.

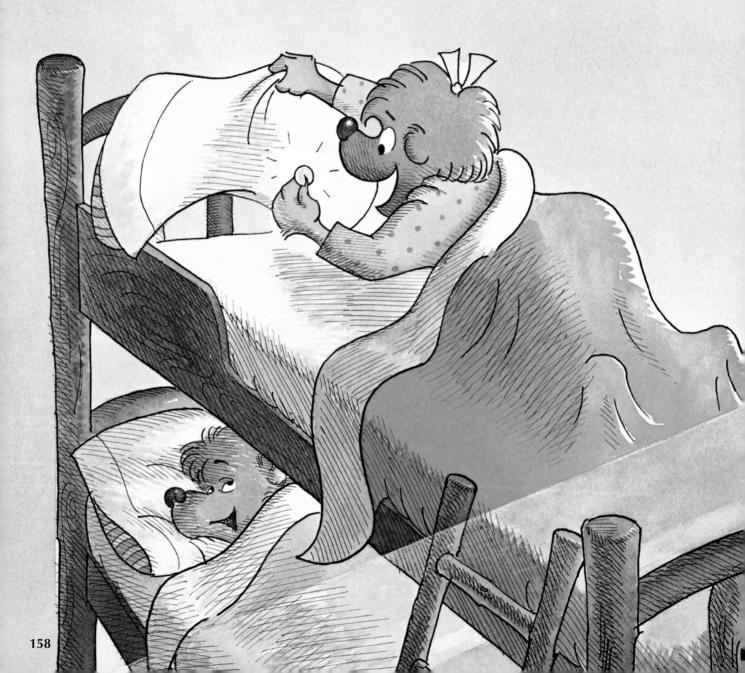

Then she ran into the
next room to show Mama
her shiny new dime.

Their stuff is all packed!
Here comes the truck!
Let's move with the Bears
And wish them good luck.

The Bear family didn't always live in the big tree house down a sunny dirt road deep in Bear Country.

Years ago, when Brother Bear was an only cub, they lived in a hillside cave halfway up Great Bear Mountain at the far edge of Bear Country.

It was a comfortable cave, cool in summer and cozy in winter. And while it wasn't perfect—it tended to be dark and it dripped and trickled a bit—it was *home*, and the Bear family was quite happy there.

Happy *and* busy.

Mama Bear kept busy managing things and tending the vegetable patch.

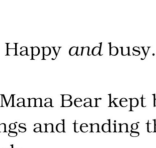

Papa Bear had plenty to do with his wood cutting and furniture making.

And Brother Bear kept busy climbing, collecting rocks, and playing with his friends.

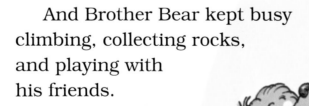

But living on the mountainside wasn't perfect—it wasn't easy growing vegetables in the thin, rocky soil, and the trees Papa needed were getting fewer and farther between. But the sun was bright, the air was clear and sparkling, and the view was *magnificent*!

Yes, the Bear family was happy and content living in their hillside cave halfway up Great Bear Mountain at the far edge of Bear Country. . . . Until one day, Papa Bear said, "My dears, the time has come to move."

"Move?" cried Brother Bear.

"That's right," said Papa. "The trees are getting few and far between on the mountainside."

"Yes," said Mama, "and it's not easy raising enough vegetables for a growing family in this thin, rocky soil."

"Where are we going to move *to*?" Brother asked.

"To the valley," said Papa as he began putting lamps and things into a box.

"The valley?" said Brother. The valley down there was nice to look at, but he wasn't so sure he wanted to live there. It was so far away.

169

"What about my toys?"
asked Brother.

"We'll take them along,
of course. Put them in here,"
said Papa, handing him a box.

"And what about my books?"

"We'll take them along, too," said Papa,
handing him another box.

"And what about my friends?" asked Brother. "We can't put *them* in a box and take them along!"

"That's true," said Mama, lifting Brother onto her lap. "You'll be leaving your friends behind. Papa and I will, too. That's what happens when you move. But you can keep in touch with them. You can write, even visit, perhaps. And besides, you can make lots of new friends."

"*When* are we going to move?" Brother wanted to know.

"Tomorrow, bright and early," Mama told him. "The moving bears will be here first thing in the morning."

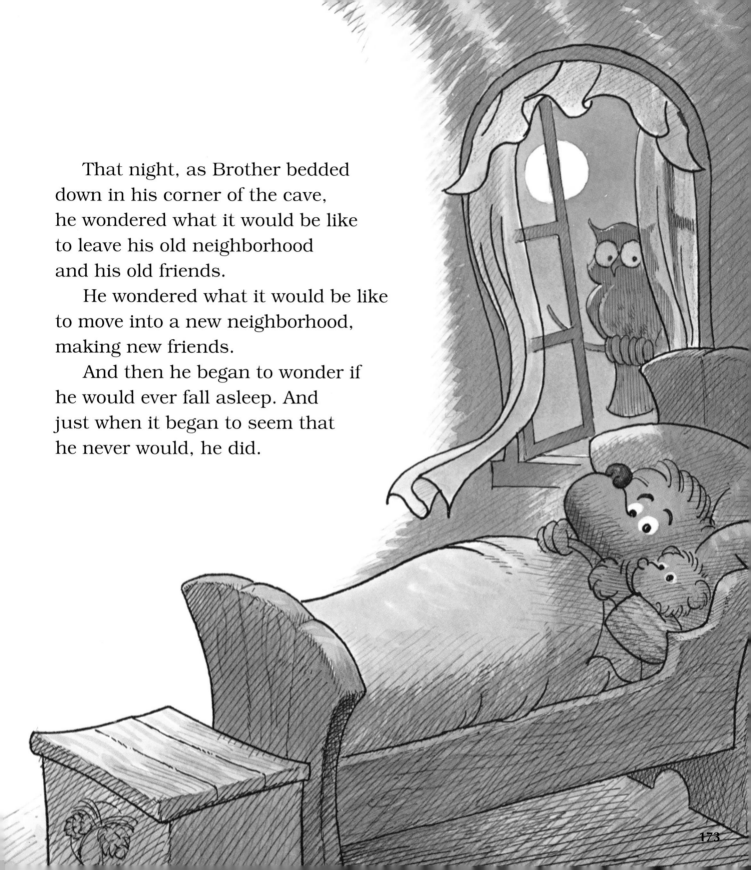

That night, as Brother bedded
down in his corner of the cave,
he wondered what it would be like
to leave his old neighborhood
and his old friends.

He wondered what it would be like
to move into a new neighborhood,
making new friends.

And then he began to wonder if
he would ever fall asleep. And
just when it began to seem that
he never would, he did.

The next morning, the moving bears came
with their big truck and began moving the
Bear family's things out of the cave.
"Everything goes!" said Papa.

And everything did.
The moving bears
were very fast, but very
careful. Before long,
the cave was empty.

Then, after a fond farewell look at their old home, the Bear family said good-bye to their friends and neighbors, got into their car, and headed down the mountain. The big moving truck followed.

Down, down the mountainside they went.
After a few tight spots and a few wrong
turns, they were in the rich green forest
of the valley.

"Look at that forest!" said Papa.
"Now I shall have plenty
of wood to cut."

They passed farms
with fine fields.

"And look at that
rich brown soil!
What a vegetable
garden I'll have!"
said Mama.

Brother was on the lookout
for friends and playmates. But
all he saw were a frog and
some butterflies. And they didn't
look very friendly.

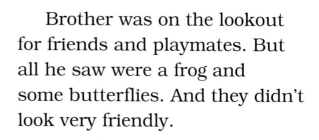

"Get ready!" said Papa, as they
turned onto a sunny dirt road.
"Just around this bend is our
new home!"

"But, it's a tree!" said Brother.

"A tree *house*!" said Papa. "A fine tree house—with a downstairs, and an upstairs, and an attic . . . and even a room of your own!"

It was indeed a fine house—a whole house hollowed out of a great oak.

It did need work—the paint was old, there were some broken steps, and some of the bark was loose—but Mama and Papa had great plans for fixing it up.

As the movers took the Bears' things into their new home, the Bears imagined what it would look like when it was all fixed.

It was going to be very beautiful.

They were so busy imagining, that they didn't notice they had company. Their new neighbors had come with gifts of welcome. There were rabbits with carrot stew, bird and squirrel families with seeds and nuts, and a number of bear families with honeycombs, wild berries—and lots of cubs to make friends with.

The Bear family felt very welcome in their new neighborhood. That night they went to bed very tired, but very happy.

And when they got their tree house all fixed up, it was just about perfect!

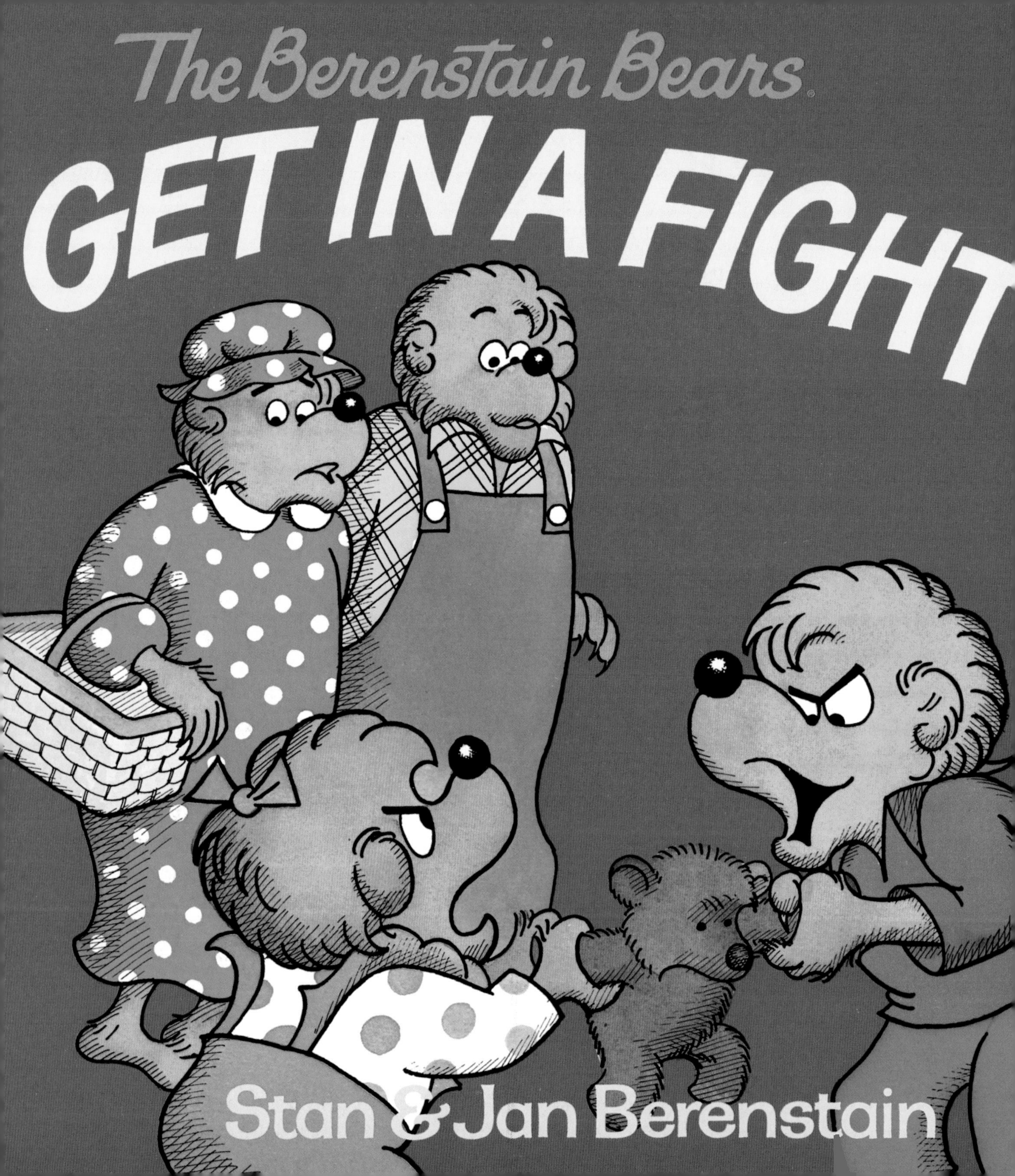
The Berenstain Bears®
GET IN A FIGHT
Stan & Jan Berenstain

When two small bears
Don't get along,
The grownups worry—
What went wrong?

Most mornings, in Bear Country, the sun rose to greet the day and the mockingbird sang its copycat songs outside an upstairs window of the bears' tree house.

And inside the tree house Brother Bear and Sister Bear would wake up.

195

Brother and Sister usually got along very well.

They took turns nicely with the bathroom.

They said "please" and "thank you" at breakfast.

They often sat together on the school bus.

And after school they worked together happily on their special project—their own backyard tree house.

197

But one gray morning Brother and Sister didn't get along well at all! Maybe it was the weather—or maybe it was because the mockingbird slept late. But whatever it was, Brother and Sister Bear got into a big fight....

Sister Bear opened her eyes and stretched. Then she sat up and let her legs dangle over the edge of her bed—right in Brother Bear's face. She didn't do it to be rude. It was just one of those things that happen with bunk beds.

But that morning Brother was not in a very good mood.

"Sister!" he shouted. "Get your dopey feet out of my face!"

"My feet aren't dopey, and they're not
in your face!" she shouted back.

"Get your dopey *face* out of my face!"
snarled Brother.

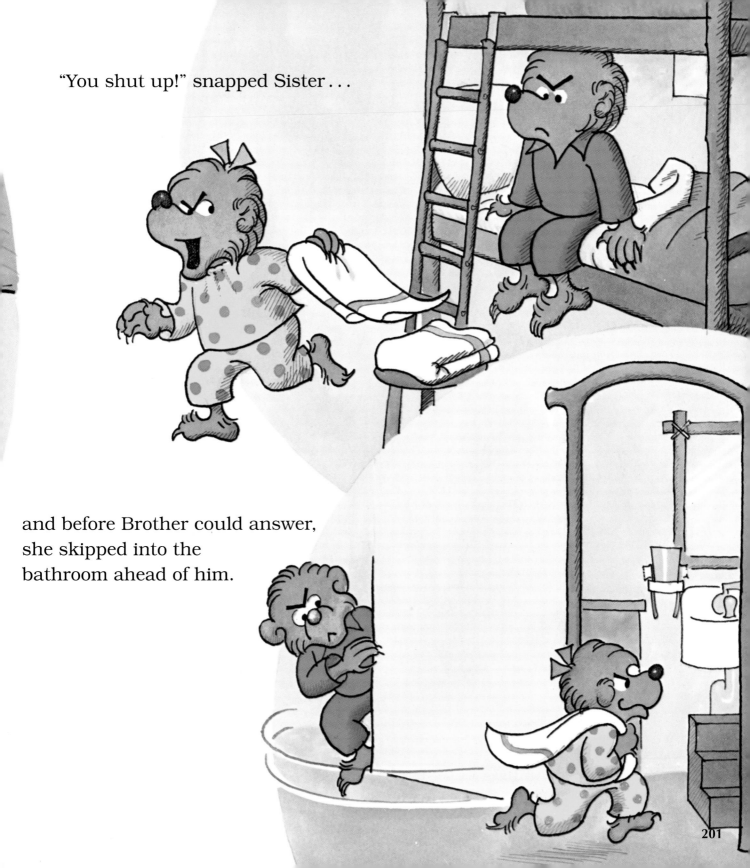

"You shut up!" snapped Sister...

and before Brother could answer,
she skipped into the
bathroom ahead of him.

She took a *very long time* . . .

brushing her teeth,

washing up,

and brushing her fur.

"You'd better come out of that bathroom!" shouted Brother, banging on the door.

"Brother Bear," said Papa, coming out of his bedroom, "you know better than to shout at your sister." "But she's taking too long in the bathroom," complained Brother, "and she's doing it on purpose!"

When Brother raised his fist to
bang on the door again, it opened
and out came Sister, all spruced up.
"Good morning, Papa,"
she said, as nice
as you please.
"Gr-r-r!"
said Brother.

Brother and Sister didn't say "please" and "thank you" that morning at breakfast—because they weren't speaking to each other.

And they didn't sit together on the school bus. Sister sat in the front and Brother sat way in the back.

That afternoon they made a line down the middle of their backyard tree house to show which half was whose. It wasn't much fun sitting up there in their tree house not speaking.

Especially when it began to rain—hard!

Later they kept on being mean by
taking back the things they usually shared.

Sister took back her modeling
clay—which Brother had made
into dinosaurs—and rolled it
into one big lump.

Brother took back his trucks and
planes and put them on the top shelf
where Sister couldn't reach them.

They got so angry that they forgot they weren't speaking and began shouting at each other even louder than before. Then Papa lost his temper and began shouting at them to stop shouting.

The neighbors didn't know which was worse—the big storm or the racket coming from the bears' house.

Mama had quite enough. She put two fingers to her mouth and whistled—*very very loudly.* Papa and the cubs were so surprised that they stopped shouting.

"I didn't know you could whistle like that, Mama," said Sister.

TWE-E-ET

"Well, I can. And I can also tell you," said Mama sternly, "that I've had quite enough of this foolish fighting. Why, I doubt you two even remember what you're fighting about!"

The cubs tried to remember, but they couldn't.

Mama took the cubs into her lap.
"Everybody gets into an argument
once in a while," she said. "Even
folks who love each
other very much."

"You and I don't have arguments," said Papa.

"Oh, yes, we do," said Mama.

"No, we don't," argued Papa.

"We're having one right now," said Mama, "about whether or not we have arguments!"

While Papa thought that one over, Mama went on to say that occasional arguments are part of living together.

"We get angry, even call each other names and say things we really don't mean—and after a while it's over."

"Like the storm?" asked Sister.
The rain had almost stopped,
and the sun was beginning to
shine through the clouds.

"Yes," said Mama. "Like the storm."
"Look!" said Papa.

The sun shining on the last of
the rain had made a rainbow.

"A rainbow is something very
beautiful that happens after a
storm," said Mama, looking at the
cubs.

"You mean like making up after
a big fight?"

"Sort of," said Mama.

So Brother and Sister Bear
hugged and made up.
And got along just beautifully—
until the next time, anyway.

# The Berenstain Bears
# GO TO CAMP

GRIZZLY BOB'S DAY CAMP

# Stan & Jan Berenstain

It was the last day of school and the beginning of vacation—that wonderful time when little bears could sit around doing absolutely nothing. Brother Bear and Sister Bear shouted good-bye to Teacher Jane and hopped onto the bus for the happy trip home.

"Well?" asked Mama Bear after a day or so of vacation. "Are you enjoying sitting around doing nothing?"

"It's great!" said Sister.

"Absolutely!" said Brother.

"There's just one trouble with it," added Sister. *"There's nothing to do!"*

"Here, take a look at this," said Mama as she reached for something that had come in the mail.

This is what it looked like:

SWIMMING

CANOEING

ARTS & CRAFTS

SPORTS & GAMES

NATURE STUDY

FULLY SUPERVISED

BOB

AND DON'T FORGET OUR EXCITING OVERNIGHT CAMPFIRE AND SLEEP-OUT

Some of the things looked interesting. But Brother wondered what "fully supervised" meant. And Sister wasn't so sure about that "overnight sleep-out." It sounded a little scary.

"Where is this camp?" asked Sister.

"Not far," answered Mama.

"How will we get there?" Brother wanted to know.

"A bus comes for you in the morning and brings you home in the afternoon."

"Sounds a little like school," said Brother.

"We'll think about it," said the cubs, and went back to doing nothing—well, not exactly nothing. . . .

They picked a few wildflowers,

chased a few butterflies,

turned over a few rocks . . .

—and thought about it.

"Mama, could we try Grizzly
Bob's Day Camp just to see if we
like it?" they asked.
"Of course," said Mama.

A couple of mornings later, Brother and Sister
were in camp shorts and T-shirts,
all ready and waiting when the bus came.

It didn't look much like
the school bus.

And Grizzly Bob
didn't look much like Teacher Jane.

And the camp didn't look
anything like school!

235

Grizzly Bob had built his camp beside a lake at the edge of the forest. There were log buildings, a flagpole flying the camp flag, a big bulletin board with the camp rules—there certainly were a lot of rules—some interesting paths, a roped-in place to swim. . . . There was even a big red canoe!

Bob had made name tags for the cubs. "You're campmates now, so you better get to know each other," he said.

Then he took them on a tour of the camp. There was an office with a desk, where he did his paperwork, and a first-aid corner full of bandages and things for cuts and bruises.

There was a Rec Hall to go into when it rained. "Rec" was short for recreation.

There was a picnic place and a barbecue pit where they roasted hot dogs for lunch. Sister burned hers a little, but she traded with another cub who liked burned hot dogs.

Bob announced that after lunch they would all climb up Spook Hill to the very top of Skull Rock— the special place where they would have their end-of-camp sleep-out.

It was quite a climb!

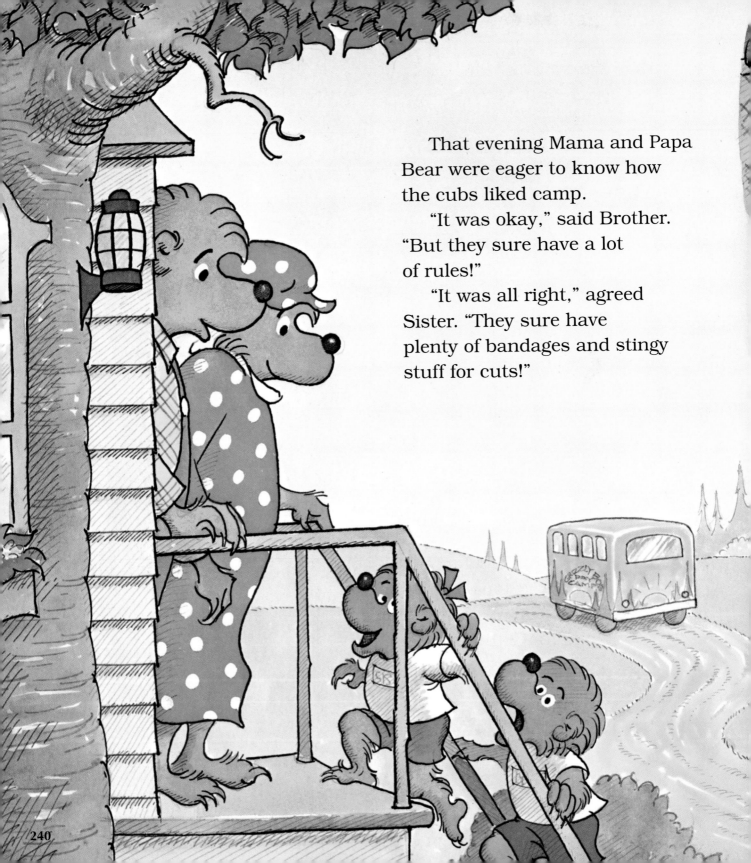

That evening Mama and Papa Bear were eager to know how the cubs liked camp.

"It was okay," said Brother. "But they sure have a lot of rules!"

"It was all right," agreed Sister. "They sure have plenty of bandages and stingy stuff for cuts!"

But what they were both thinking about was Skull Rock and that end-of-camp sleep-out.

Especially Sister.

The second day was different. Brother had a great day. He passed the swimming test and was allowed to ride in the canoe.

Sister didn't have such a good day. She played dodge ball and some of the cubs threw pretty hard.

The third day Sister had
fun. She got a star for a
birch picture frame she
made in arts and crafts.
But Brother hurt his knee
in the wheelbarrow race.

The fourth day both
of them had fun—

244

And every day after that! So
much fun that they forgot
about Skull Rock and
the sleep-out . . .

—almost.

Papa found the sleeping bags that he and Mama had used on their honeymoon, and when the camp bus came on the morning of the big night, Brother and Sister were ready . . . sort of.

The climb up Spook Hill wasn't so hard this time—even with backpacks. The cubs were strong and tough from their summer of camping. Tomorrow would be Field Day—the last day of camp, when their parents would come to watch their games and contests and see awards given out. But, for now, all the cubs could think about was the big sleep-out.

It was just beginning to get dark when they reached Skull Rock.

Grizzly Bob built a campfire. Then
he went into a small cave. When he came
out, he was dressed in an old-fashioned
costume!

Then the cubs sat in a semicircle,
and the storytime began.

Bob told them old legends of the great animals—the story of the Great Grizzly as Big as a Mountain, the Soaring Eagle Who Filled the Sky, and the Mighty Salmon Whose Colors Made the Rainbow.

As Bob told the old stories, the cubs could almost see the wonderful creatures in the firelit smoke as it curled up into the night sky.

After the campfire, they had cocoa
and honey bread. Then they curled up
in their sleeping bags. And soon they
were all fast asleep . . . even Sister.

The next day Brother
and Sister did very well
in the Field Day games
and contests.

Brother won a trophy for finishing second
in the dash, and Sister got medals for the
dead-bear's float and for her bead belt.

It was almost the end of summer; school
would be starting in a couple of weeks.

"Well?" asked Papa. "How did you like camp?"

"It was great!" said Brother, hugging his
trophy.

"It was great!" agreed Sister, wearing her medals
proudly. "But you know something? After Grizzly
Bob's Day Camp, school will be like a vacation!"

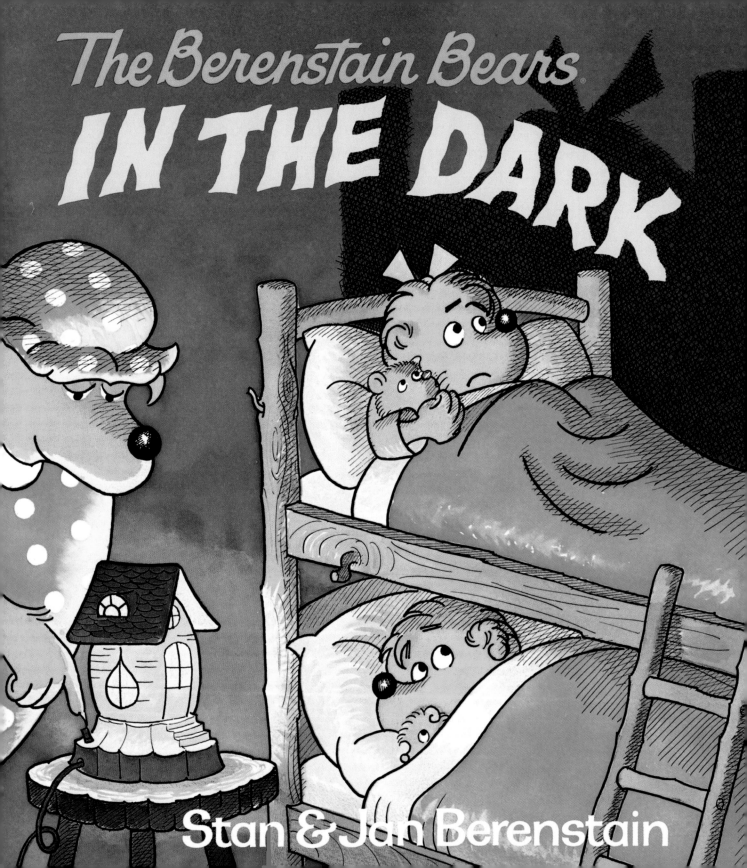

Being afraid
of the dark
Doesn't just happen
to you.
It happens,
sometimes,
To little bears, too.

"Brother Bear," said Sister impatiently, "are you going to take all day to pick your books?"

Sister and Brother Bear were at the Bear Country Library. Sister had already chosen her books and was waiting at the check-out desk.

"Hold your horses," said Brother. "I'm looking for a good mystery."

OUT

CUBS CORNER

MYSTERIES

Sister Bear usually took out storybooks and books about nature—and sometimes books of poems. Brother liked those, too, but lately he'd become interested in mysteries—especially spooky ones.

"Hey, this one looks good," he said finally. "Okay, let's check out."

"Hmmm," said Sister, looking at the cover. It was called *The Case of the Crying Cave*. "It looks scary to me!"

"Say! This is really good!"
said Brother later that evening
when the Bear family had settled
down for some reading. "Would you
like me to read it to you?" he asked
Sister.

Sister was looking at a storybook
about three kittens who were arguing
about which was the prettiest—
and it *was* a little boring.

"Or are you scared?" teased Brother.
"Of course not," said Sister. She left
her book on the floor and climbed onto
the bench to sit beside him.

The mystery began quietly. It told
about some bear scouts who were on
an overnight camp-out.

"A mysterious cave!" said the bear scouts. "We should explore it!"

But before the scouts could go into the cave a wailing sound came from the cave.

WHOO-O-O-O

It was a strange sound and it frightened the scouts. "Help!" they cried.

O-O-O-O

When the scouts discovered a dark, secret cave, Brother's mystery began to get a little exciting. And when the cave began to cry and wail, it was anything but quiet!

"*'Who-o-o-o-o!* cried the deep, dark mysterious cave,'" read Brother with a lot of expression. "*'Who-o-o-o-o!'*"

"Stop!" said Sister, putting her fingers in her ears. "That's enough!" And she went back to her storybook.

"Scaredy bear! Scaredy bear!" teased Brother.

"And that's quite enough of *that*," added Papa Bear, looking up from his paper.

At the cubs' bedtime Papa and Mama said good night, turned off the light, and left the cubs in the usual sleepy darkness.

Outside the tree house the bright, busy sounds of day had given way to the soft, soothing sounds of night—the quiet conversation of frogs and toads, the soft cry of the owl, the sigh of the night wind. And if you listened very hard, you could *almost* hear the softest sound of all—the sound of lightning bugs switching their lights on and off, on and off.

But inside the tree house Sister
Bear wasn't even beginning to fall
asleep. That night the dark didn't
seem the least bit quiet and sleepy.
In fact, it seemed like the spooky
darkness of a scary cave. And the
friendly old chest of drawers and
funny clothes tree that Papa had
made didn't seem so friendly and
funny. They seemed more like
cave creatures.

So when Brother decided to
tease her a little more by
making a wailing noise—a
really spooky wailing noise—
it gave her quite a scare.

"Mama! Papa!" she cried.
"Hurry! Come quick!"

And come quickly they did.

Papa rushed into the dark room and tripped over the clothes tree.

Mama rushed in after Papa and tripped over him.

In the commotion Sister fell out of bed and landed on both of them!

Then Brother, who had started it all with his spooky wail, turned on the light. What a mess! Sister, still scared, was holding on to Papa. Papa was holding on to the toe he had stubbed. And Mama was looking for the nightcap she had lost in the confusion. All three of them were pretty annoyed with Brother Bear.

It turned out to be a very long night in the Bears' tree house. Papa and Mama tried to explain that there was nothing to be afraid of in the dark (except maybe running into a clothes tree and stubbing your toe)—but it didn't do any good.

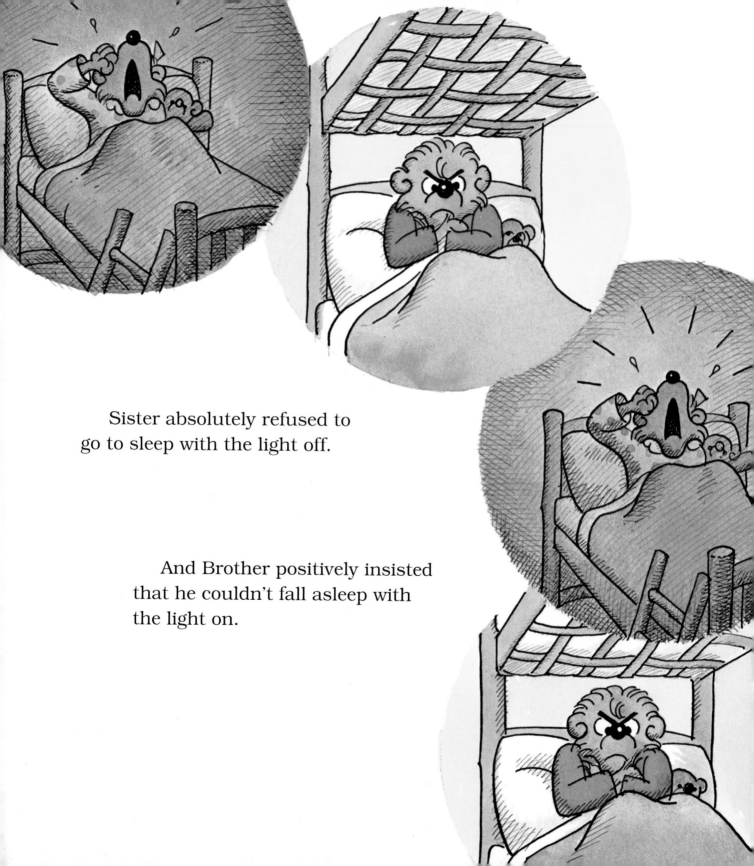

Sister absolutely refused to go to sleep with the light off.

And Brother positively insisted that he couldn't fall asleep with the light on.

The next morning the Bear family was very sleepy-eyed.

"Boy," said Brother, yawning, "I sure don't want to go through another night like that!"

"Neither do I," said Papa. "And I think I have an idea that might help."

He took Sister's hand. "Come with me," he said.

"Where are we going?" she wanted to know.

"Up to the attic."

"The attic? But it's dark in the attic—even in the daytime."

"I know," said Papa. "But there's something I want to show you. Anyway, there's nothing so special about the dark. It's just part of nature, like the light. It's your imagination that makes the dark seem spooky sometimes."

"What's imagination?" asked Sister.

"Imagination is what makes us think that chests of drawers and clothes trees are cave creatures."

"I wish I didn't have one," said Sister.

"Don't say that," said Papa. "A lively imagination is one of the best things a cub can have. It's imagination that lets us paint pictures, make up poems, invent inventions! The trick is to take charge of your imagination—and not let it take charge of you."

When they got to the attic,
Papa began to rummage
through boxes, looking for
something.

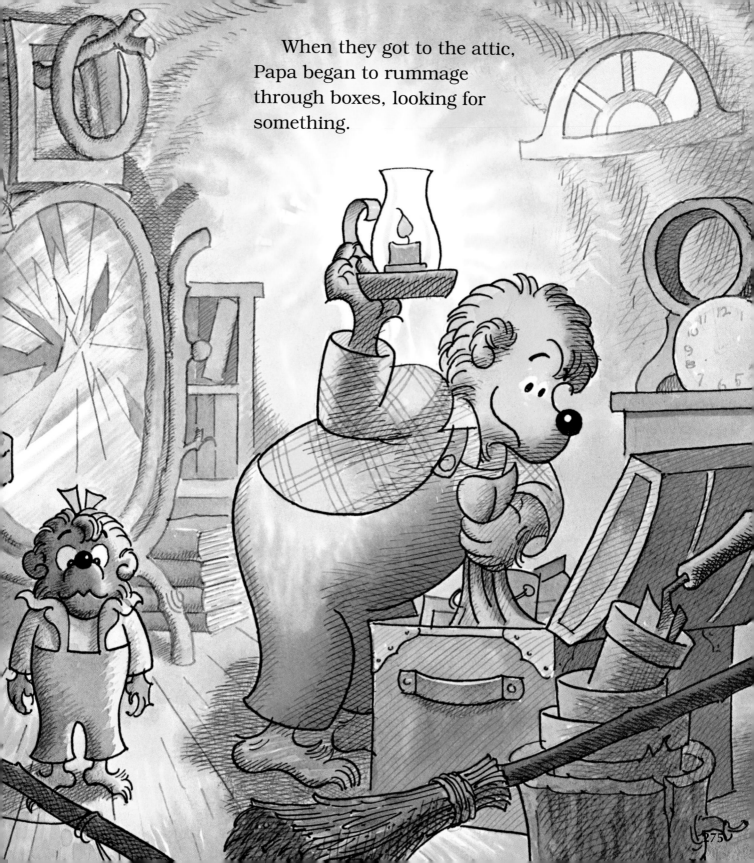

Sister tried to follow
Papa's advice and not let her
imagination take charge.

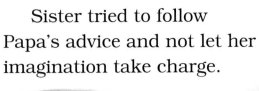

And it worked—a spooky
shape turned out to be the
shadow of some old tools.

What looked like a giant
was really some piled-up
furniture.

"Here it is!" said Papa. "My old night light!
The one I used when I was a cub and had a little
trouble falling asleep in the dark!"

Sister couldn't quite believe that her big,
powerful papa was ever afraid of the dark.

"Oh, sure," said Papa. "Most of us are at one
time or another."

"How about reading the rest of *The Case of the Crying Cave*?" Sister asked Brother later that day.

"Are you sure you want me to?"

"Sure! I want to see how it turns out!" she insisted.

When it turned out that there was nothing very spooky about the terrible wailing noise (it was caused by wind blowing across an opening in the roof of the cave—like the noise you make when you blow across the top of a bottle), Sister was a little disappointed.

"Why?" asked Brother.

"Because," she said, "I was hoping the wailing would be a really spooky, scary monster!" And she leaned down from her bunk over Brother's and made a spooky, scary monster face at him.

"*Cut that out!*" cried Brother.

Then Sister went right to sleep.
But Brother lay awake for quite
some time listening to the owl
hoots and thinking that maybe
he'd had enough mysteries for
a while.

# The Berenstain Bears
## and the
# MESSY ROOM

TRASH

## Stan & Jan Berenstain

When small bears forget
To pick up, store and stash,
Some of their favorite things
End up in the trash.

From the outside, the Bears' tree house, which stood beside a sunny dirt road deep in Bear Country, looked very neat and well-kept.

The flower beds sparkled with red, yellow, and blue tulips.

The woodwork was freshly painted and in good repair.

The grass was cut and the vegetable patch was properly weeded.

Even the bird's nest that perched on one of the tree house branches was well-trimmed.

The inside of the Bears' tree house was neat and clean too.

The pictures were straight.

The piano was dusted.

The kitchen was spick-and-span.

Even the basement was neat and clean.
(And if you think it's easy to keep a
tree house basement neat and clean—
well, you've never tried to do it!)

Yes, the Bears' tree house was a
lesson in neatness and cleanliness.

Except for one place…

Brother Bear and Sister Bear's room.
IT…WAS…A…*MESS*!!!

A dust-catching, wall-to-wall, helter-skelter mess!

A half-done jigsaw puzzle gathered dust in one corner of the room.

A group of Brother's dinosaur models collected cobwebs in another.

Sister's stuffed animals were everywhere.

It wasn't that Brother and Sister were naturally messy. They *tried* to keep their room straight.

They made their beds...

most of the time,

and they swept
and picked up…

once in a while.

The trouble was that when clean-up time came, they spent more time arguing than cleaning.

"How am *I* supposed to sweep with your dumb dinosaur toys all over the floor?" argued Sister.

"They're not toys—they're *models*! And don't move them! I'm working on a set-up of the Pleistocene Age!" Brother protested.

"Pleistocene schmeistocene!" shouted Sister.

Not only was Brother and Sister's room a mess, but Brother and Sister were getting to be a mess too—always arguing about clean-up chores instead of sharing the job and working as a team.

What usually happened was that while the cubs
argued about whose turn it was to do what,
Mama took the broom and did the sweeping herself...

and she often did the picking up too.
That was the worst part—the picking up.

*And* the putting away.

Well, the mess just seemed to build up and build up, until one day . . . maybe it was because Mama's back was a little stiff, or maybe it was stepping on Brother's airplane cement, or maybe she was just fed up with that messy room, but whatever it was . . . Mama Bear lost her temper!

She stormed into the cubs' room with a big box.

"The first thing we have to do is get rid of all this junk!" she said.

"*JUNK!?*" said Brother and Sister, watching in horror as Mama began to throw things into the box.

"My Teddy isn't junk!" screamed Sister.

"My bird's nest collection isn't junk!" yelled Brother at the top of his lungs.

The screaming and yelling got
so loud that it reached Papa,
who was in his workshop putting
the finishing touches on a batch
of chairs that had been ordered
by one of his customers. He
couldn't imagine what was wrong.

He hurried up the stairs and looked into the messy, *noisy* room. It didn't take a deep thinker to figure out what was going on.

307

Papa got Mama's and the cubs'
attention and called a family meeting
right then and there.

"Now, the mess has really built up in this
room," he said. "In fact, it's the worst case
of messy build-up I've ever seen!

"And it isn't fair," he continued. "It isn't
fair to your mama and me, because we have a lot
of other things to take care of. And it isn't
fair to you, because you really can't have fun
or relax in a room that's such a terrible mess."

"But Mama is putting all my things into that box—even my Teddy!" said Sister.

"And my things too!" cried Brother.

Then Papa got an idea.

"A box, yes," he said. "Better yet, a lot of different kinds of boxes— a big toy box for your large toys... I can make one for you in my shop... and some smaller boxes for your collections and models."

"And how about one of those boards with holes and pegs to hang things on?" asked Sister.

"A pegboard!" said Papa. "Great idea! All this room needs is a little organization."

"A little organization—*and* a few rules!" added Mama. "Rules about more sweeping and less arguing and not leaving things to gather dust and cobwebs."

Papa set to work making
a fine big toy box and a
large pegboard . . .

while the cubs and Mama
sorted out toys, books, games,
and puzzles and put them
into boxes that fit neatly
into the closet.
Every box was
clearly labeled.

Some of the cubs' things did end up in Mama's big throwaway box— not Sister's Teddy, of course, but some of Brother's bird's nests (the crumbling, falling-apart ones).

It was a very big job cleaning up all that messy build-up. But after a lot of straightening up and putting away, the job was finally finished.

"Wow!" said Brother. "That was quite a job, but it was worth it!"

"It looks like a whole new room!" said Sister.

The cubs were right.

STORAGE STORAGE

STICKERS TAPE PASTE CRAYONS PENCILS

STONES CARDS MAGIC TRICKS PAINTS

SHELLS FEATHERS STRING CHALK

DISHES CLAY

MINI DOLLS MODEL KITS

DOLL CLOTHES DINOSAURS ROCKS

PAPER DOLLS BLOCKS

YARN CLOTH

GAMES SPORTS EQUIPMENT

PUZZLES

DINO- SAURS

And Papa had been right too. It was so much more enjoyable to live in a neat, clean, well-organized room— and so much more relaxing!

It wasn't as exciting to open the big storage closet now, but it was much more practical—and a lot more fun!

# THE END

BERENSTAIN BEARS®